THE STREAM TEAM

By Kevin Miller

www.bakkenbooks.com

The Stream Team by Kevin Miller
Copyright © 2024 Bakken Books

All rights reserved. This book is protected under the copyright laws of the United States of America. This book may not be copied or reprinted for commercial gain or profit. This book is a work of fiction. The Game On series is a work of fiction. Names, characters, businesses, places, events, incidents, and other locales are either the products of the author's imagination or used in a fictitious manner. Any resemblance to actual persons, living or dead, or actual events is purely coincidental.

ISBN: 978-1-955657-97-6
Published by Bakken Books
For Worldwide Distribution
Printed in the USA

www.bakkenbooks.com

Other Bakken Books Stories

Camping books for kids

Mystery books for kids

Hunting books for kids

Fishing books for kids

www.bakkenbooks.com

Math adventures for kids

History adventures for kids

Space adventures for kids

Humorous adventures for kids

It was the word "job" that first put the idea into my head. That is, it was the threat of having to *get* a job, as in . . .

"That's it, Wyatt. No more loafing around the house for you this summer. It's time to get yourself a job—a J-O-B. I don't care if it's cutting grass at the golf course, stocking shelves at the grocery store, or cleaning rooms at the hotel, but you're going to do something to earn your keep around here. Understand?"

That's my mom speaking, in case it isn't clear from the tone, although it could just as easily have been my dad. Both of them had been on my case lately to "do something with my life." It was only early January, but they were already planning my summer—planning to make it miserable, that is. Their idea of a New Year's resolution, I guess.

The thing is, I was *already* doing something with my life, or at least I thought I was. My parents just didn't see the value in it—not yet, anyway.

What was the thing I was doing, the activity that occupied every waking moment of my day when I wasn't focused on schoolwork, doing chores, avoiding my little sister, or listening to my parents lecture me about how I was wasting my life? Come on—it was 2024, I was a fourteen-year-old boy, and I had a high-speed Internet connection wired straight into my house. What else could it be?

Gaming!

It didn't matter what type of game we were talking about—shooters, sandboxes, platformers, battle royales, driving games, sports games, MMOs, MOBAs, or MMORPGs—if it involved battling someone else for fame and glory, I was in.

My ultimate dream? To become a full-time

THE STREAM TEAM

gamer just like my heroes—strike it rich, live in a mansion, own a fleet of cars, and live stream to my millions of adoring fans. There was no way I was going to become a drone who went off to do some mindless job each day just to earn money. And I knew if I gave in to my parents' demands and got a summer job, it wouldn't be long before I was stuck in the same depressing rut as everybody else. But I didn't want to be like everybody else; I wanted to be a *somebody*. And there was one game that I knew could make that happen.

Rumble Royale.

I'm not sure what it is about that game, but from the moment I first played it, something clicked. Whether looting materials, building, editing, or battling, there were few people I couldn't beat—at least when I was playing for fun.

The cool thing about *Rumble Royale* is that the game offers all sorts of opportunities to enter online tournaments, where players can win real money right from the comfort of their own homes. Then they can go on to win bigger and better tournaments—and even more money—at huge, invitation-only events. What could be better than that?

The problem was, as good as I was at the game, the moment money was on the line, something inside me went haywire. My hands started to sweat, my heart began to pound, and my normally ironclad decision-making skills went out the window.

I turned into a total noob.

A bot.

"What are you doing?" my anonymous playing partners would often yell at me in exasperation, their voices causing me to cringe in humiliation as they blasted through my headset. "Why don't you do us all a favor and just jump off the map?"

Ouch.

The worst part was I was still good, but I was never quite good enough. As the safe zone got smaller and the fighting became more intense, it was like I forgot everything that had gotten me that far. Try as I might, I'd always finish just outside the rankings. All that money up for grabs but always just out of reach.

It was painful.

I won't bother telling you how many of my video game controllers suffered as a result of my failures. Let's just say they were on my birthday and Christmas wish lists almost every year.

The more I raged at my inability to break through to the big time, the more convinced my parents became that video games weren't the solution to my problems; they *were* the problem. I still thought video games were my ticket to the big leagues, but the time to prove that was running out. So, with summer just six months away and my parents hounding me to get a job—which would reduce my gaming time to nearly zero, not to mention crush my soul under a mountain of boredom and hopelessness—I had to do something fast.

As I struggled to come up with a plan, I realized that up until then, I had been trying to make it on my own. But when I looked at my gaming heroes, nearly all of them had one thing in common—they had made it big as part of a team.

That made perfect sense. Not only could teammates rely on each other, revive each other, and watch each other's backs, there were way more opportunities to play tournaments and win in *Rumble Royale* as part of a duo or a four-person squad than there were if I tried to make it playing solo.

So, with that thought in mind, I decided it was time to come in from the cold, lonely fringes of the *Rumble Royale* world and recruit my own squad. If I could do that and we could win some actual money playing the game, maybe, just maybe, my parents would finally get off my back and put this whole J-O-B thing to rest.

The question was, where was I supposed to start looking?

- 2 -

When it came to finding potential teammates, I concluded that I had two main options— OL or IRL, a.k.a. cyberspace or meatspace. If you still don't get it, or if you're a parent reading this, that means *online* or *in real life.*

I also had to think about whether I should make my recruiting efforts public or keep them a secret. If I recruited players online, I could hide behind my gamertag, *KwyattWyatt*—I know. Pretty clever, right? But sooner or later, potential teammates would ask to see my stats so they could determine how good I was, and seeing as I had yet to win a single tournament, I didn't have much to show for myself. Plus, anyone who was any good was already part of a team. It wasn't like there was a waiting room full of future champions just sitting around waiting to be snapped up by some noob like me.

Recruiting in the real world came with its own set of problems, though. First of all, because I spent most of my time holed up in my gaming room with my eyes glued to my slick three-monitor setup, I didn't have a whole lot of friends to draw on. Plus, the few friends I did have were terrible at video games.

Second, because I was worried that people would make fun of me, I hadn't told anyone about my dream of making it big as a professional gamer. Even though most kids were into gaming and watched the same streamers on Twitch, YouTube, Mixer, and TikTok as I did, I knew that the moment I announced I wanted to become one of them, I'd be laughed right out of my school. I don't know why that is, but for some reason, the moment someone wants to do something different, people start lining up to cut them down.

So, it seemed like no matter which way I went

about things, this whole team-building campaign might be over before it began.

Then another idea struck me. Instead of scouting people who were *already* good at *Rumble Royale*, why not find some potential teammates who had no experience with the game whatsoever but had the skills needed to become a champion and then train them instead?

That seemed like a great plan. Not only would it eliminate the need to advertise, it wouldn't matter that all the good players online had already been taken. But where could I find such people, and how would I recognize them when I did?

As I pondered that problem, I made a list of all the qualities I could think of that were required to be a good *Rumble Royale* player. Like most video games, I figured it came down to five things:

- Fast reflexes
- Excellent hand-eye coordination
- Top-notch problem-solving skills
- A desire to win at any cost
- The discipline to practice, practice, practice

Oh, and considering my smashed controllers, sweaty palms, and pounding heart whenever cold, hard cash was on the line, I realized there was a sixth vital skill:

- The ability to stay cool under pressure.

Now that I had my list, all I had to do was find three people who already had those qualities, sell them on the dream of making it big as part of a professional video game team, and then put them through a rigorous training program to make them *Rumble Royale* superstars. All in a matter or six months or less.

No problem, right?

- 3 -

To keep things simple, I decided to start with the first two items on my list—fast reflexes and excellent hand-eye coordination. After doing some research on the sports that require those skills and comparing them to the clubs available at my school, my first destination became obvious immediately.

Just my luck, it was a Tuesday, and that club practiced in the gym every Tuesday and Thursday after school. As soon as the bell rang to signal the end of classes for the day, off to the gym I went.

As I approached, my ears were met by the pinging and ponging of . . . you guessed it . . . ping-pong balls, as the table tennis club members batted them back and forth across a half-dozen green tables set up across the cavernous space. I had no idea who was the best player in the group, but I was determined to approach whoever that person happened to be.

Even though I knew next to nothing about table tennis, I could tell right away that some players were terrible, barely able to keep up a rally for more than a few hits. A handful of players were good, and others were really good, but one player stood out above all the others. In fact,

THE STREAM TEAM

---

she was sensational. Forehand, backhand, behind the back, between the legs—it didn't matter. Not a single shot got past her. And when it came to returning her shots, it looked impossible. Somehow she could use her paddle to spin the ball in any direction she wanted. The moment it hit the table, there was no way for her opponent to tell which way it would bounce, and it always seemed to go in exactly the opposite direction of what they expected, sending them diving and sprawling across the gym's hardwood floor.

As good as she was, when it came to recruiting her as part of my *Rumble Royale* team, I could already see a complication looming. If you don't know what it was, pay attention to two keywords I just used in the preceding sentence—"she" and "her." My top candidate in the reflexes and hand-eye coordination category was a girl?

Not quite what I was expecting.

Don't get me wrong—I have no problem with girls. In fact, I'm a huge fan. But video games are usually a guy thing, especially third-person shooters like *Rumble Royale*. So, even if our school's star table tennis player had the qualities I was looking for, what were the chances she would even want to play?

Like so many other things in life, I figured there was only one way to find out.

I waited until she finished her game—she demolished her opponent 11-0—and then I approached her with a smile and a wave, hoping I looked friendly and not like I was a creeper trying to hit on her or something—which I definitely wasn't, even though she was kind of pretty.

To my relief, she smiled and waved back, but almost as soon as I started into my sales pitch, which began with me complimenting her insane table tennis skills, she held up her hand to stop me. I was confused until she pulled out her phone and typed something into it, holding her screen toward me afterward so I could read it.

"'No good English,'" I said, reading aloud the first line of what was written on the screen. Then I realized she had used a translation app to type it. "'Exchange student from China,'" I continued. I looked up at her in surprise and despair, my entire body feeling like it was beginning to wilt. "Oh, so you're not from around here?"

Massive understatement.

At that moment, all my hopes drained out of me like dirty water from a bathtub. So far, not only was my top prospect a girl, she was also from China, which meant she was probably leaving at the end of the school year, and her English was practically non-existent. Everything in me said I should just turn around and walk right out of there, hoping no one noticed my tail tucked between my legs, but then she smiled and nodded, pointing at herself.

"Shu Wang," she said, which I assumed was her name. "And you?"

Walking out on her at that point would have been downright rude, so I forced out a smile and pointed my thumb at my chest. "My name is Wyatt. Nice to meet you." She seemed startled by my response, which confused me until I realized I was talking louder than usual, as if that would help her understand me. "Sorry," I said, lowering my voice to a more normal level. "Hard of hearing." I pointed to my right ear. It was a lie, but I hoped she didn't understand that part.

"Want play?" she asked, holding up her table tennis paddle.

"Oh, no. I really shouldn't," I said. "I'm not part of the club."

"Since when does that matter?" a gruff voice said from behind me. I turned around to find the table tennis coach, Mr. Daviduke, bearing down on me. He was one of the most feared teachers in the school. His craggy face looked even more fierce due to a thick brown mustache that he had sported long before "Movember" ever became a thing. Combined with his shaved head, which glistened under the gym's halogen lights, it made him appear like an outlaw biker itching for a fight. "We're always looking for fresh meat, and as you can see, Shu could use some competition."

I turned to look at the player she had just pounded into oblivion. Seizing on the distraction, he had snuck away with his tail between his legs, just as I had been about to do.

"But I've hardly ever played before," I protested.

THE STREAM TEAM

"You can learn." Mr. Daviduke thrust a table tennis paddle into my hand, causing me to flinch in pain. "And you won't find a better teacher than Shu. Isn't that right, Shu?"

She looked at me and smiled, nodding vigorously.

Feeling trapped, I held up the paddle and considered it for a moment, then set it on the table and backed away. "Thanks, but no thanks," I said, turning to go.

Just then, I felt someone tap my shoulder. I turned back and saw Shu holding up her index finger while she used her other hand to type something into her phone. I stared, awestruck. She was even more amazing at typing than she was at table tennis. Her thumb was a blur as it raced across the screen. Then she held her phone up.

"'If no want play, why talk to me?'" I said, reading her words out loud once again, my face turning red in response to her question. "May I?" I asked, reaching for her phone. When she gave it to me, I typed out a short version of my video game pitch—taking way longer with two thumbs than she would have taken with one—then handed the phone back to her, hoping the app would do a halfway decent job of translating what I'd written.

Shu frowned as she read my message. Then her thumb flew across her phone's screen as if she were trying to set a new world record. When she was done, she handed her phone back to me.

You try my game, I try yours, it said. I looked up at her and smiled. "Sounds fair to me."

"Not so fast," Mr. Daviduke said, his iron grip clamping onto my forearm as I reached for the ping-pong paddle. I froze in place and looked up at him like a frightened animal caught in a leghold trap.

"Sir?"

His face was hard, and his eyebrows, which were nearly as thick as his mustache, were squished together above his steely eyes like two caterpillars that were ready to leap out and latch onto my face. "You break it, you buy it. Got it, Wyatt?"

If it were any other teacher, I would have laughed and pointed out his unintentional rhyme between "Wyatt" and "buy it," but considering the wild look in his eyes, I decided to let it slide.

"Yes, sir."

Then his face broke into a wide-toothed grin, which was even scarier than his frown, and his grip on my arm relaxed. Just as I was wondering whether my arm was ever going to regain its feeling, he clapped me on the back so hard that if I had been wearing false teeth, they would have popped right out of my mouth.

"Have fun out there, but don't come crying to me when she beats you." He jabbed his thick index finger into my puny pectoral muscle to emphasize that last point.

"Uh, yes, sir," I said, rubbing my throbbing chest while sneaking a glance at Shu's grinning face. She seemed to be enjoying herself far more than I would have liked. "I won't."

- 4 -

I won't bother telling you how that table tennis game went. Let's just say that by the time it was over, I didn't think Shu would ever wipe the smile off her face. Even though she knew I was a newbie, she showed me no mercy. Lightning-fast reflexes *and* a killer instinct. Despite my earlier concerns, I already liked where this was headed.

As for Mr. Daviduke, he was so disappointed in my performance that he probably would have been happier if I *had* broken his precious paddle. Then he would have had a good reason to yell at me. I wouldn't have been surprised if he wanted to break the paddle himself—right over my head.

"What now?" Shu asked once she had proven her supremacy at table tennis yet again, as if anyone in that gym doubted her abilities.

Good question, I thought. *What now?* I couldn't just invite her over to my house, could I? After all, she was from China. Did girls ever visit strange boys' houses over there?

Not knowing how else to introduce her to *Rumble Royale,* I asked for her phone and typed out an invitation, cringing in fear as I handed it back to her, afraid that she might storm out of the gym in a rage, offended that I would dare to ask such a thing. Instead, after she read the message, she smiled.

"Sure," she said, rubbing her stomach. "I'm hungry."

Hungry. Right. I was sure we had some sort of snack food at home. What did people snack on in China, anyway? Hopefully, we would have something that satisfied her.

When we got home, wouldn't you know it—my little sister, Olivia, and my mom were in the kitchen, baking cinnamon buns. The house smelled marvelous. The second my mom saw Shu come in the door behind me, her eyes lit up.

"Wyatt, you brought a friend home? How wonderful!"

I almost never brought friends home, even though my parents kept encouraging me to do so, so you can understand why she was excited.

"A *girl*friend?" Olivia said in a singsong voice, grinning her little face off.

THE STREAM TEAM

"No. And shut up," I hissed, glancing at Shu and hoping she didn't know that word.

As for Shu, she just smiled and shook my mom's flour-covered hand, bowing slightly.

"I'm Mrs. Kelsey," Mom said. "And you are...?"

"Shu. Shu Wang." She bowed her head again. This time Mom repeated the gesture.

"Shoe? As in, basketball shoe?" Olivia asked, raising one eyebrow as she gave our visitor a once-over.

"No, *shoo*— as in, get out of here," I said.

"You can't kick me out of my own kitchen!" Olivia said, putting her hands on her hips in defiance and sending up a small cloud of flour in the process. "Besides, I'm helping Mom, which is more than you ever do around here."

"Whatever," I replied. "Speaking of which, Mom, would you mind if Shu and I each had one of these?" I licked my lips as I pointed at the tray of fresh cinnamon buns smothered in cream cheese frosting, my favorite.

"*Shu* can have one," Olivia said, detaching a cinnamon bun from the others and popping it onto a plate. "As for you..."

"Of course you can *both* have one," Mom said, nudging Olivia with her elbow and frowning at her for being impolite in front of our guest. Then she cranked out a smile for Shu. "Would you like some milk as well?" She looked at Shu for a response. Judging from the expression on Shu's face, I could tell she had no idea what Mom was asking, so I opened the fridge and pulled out the milk carton.

"Milk," I said as I pointed back and forth between the carton and the cinnamon bun. "Do you want some of this with that?"

Shu nodded vigorously. I still wasn't sure about her potential as a *Rumble Royale* player, but if that or table tennis didn't work out, I was sure she had some serious potential as a professional bobblehead.

"She doesn't speak English very well," I explained. "At least, not yet."

"No wonder she's hanging out with you," Olivia murmured. "She has no idea what a dorkasaurus you are—at least, not yet." She grinned at her so-called cleverness as my mom shushed her.

With our cinnamon buns and cold glasses of milk in hand, we broke free of my mom and Olivia's banter and went downstairs to my gaming room. It was actually our basement rec room, but my parents had allowed me to take it over and turn it into a gaming utopia, a fact that irritated Olivia to no end.

"Uh, we'd better eat these first," I said, pointing to the cinnamon buns and doing my best to mime eating them. I had some strict rules when it came to my gaming setup, and number one was that no food or drink was allowed anywhere near it except water, and even that had to be in one of those bottles with a sealed sport top that allowed you to squirt water into your mouth, no exceptions.

Shu nodded in response, her cheeks already bulging with a mouthful of cinnamon bun. I didn't know if she understood me or not, but it didn't matter. She appeared to be too wrapped up in looking around my gaming room to even think about sitting at my desk.

I guess this is a good time to mention that my gaming room was pretty sick. Not only did I have a three-monitor system—one for gaming, one for chatting with my friends on Discord, and the other for watching my favorite streamers as I waited to load into a game—but I also had a 65-inch flat-screen TV mounted on the wall above my monitors. Plus, my walls and ceiling were covered with all sorts of RGB lights—bars, hexagons, triangles, you name it. I could program them into tons of cool configurations, making them all the same color or causing them to morph from one color to the next. I could even make them change in time with the music playing through my speakers if I wanted. Oliva constantly begged me to let her use the room for a dance party with her friends, but there was no way I was going to let a bunch of sixth graders in there unsupervised.

"Cool room," Shu said, swallowing the mouthful of cinnamon bun she had been chewing and then taking another bite.

"Uh, thanks," I replied, glad she was impressed.

"Where game?" she asked, looking around.

"Here, I'll show you." I set my cinnamon bun and milk aside and slid into my gaming chair. As hungry as I was after our table tennis match, and as delicious as that cinnamon bun looked and smelled, it would have to wait. Like I said, when it came to food and drink and my gaming setup, there were no exceptions, not even for me.

As Shu watched, I booted up *Rumble Royale*. Thankfully, it didn't take long for the lobby to fill, and soon my avatar was in the War Wagon, flying toward the map.

"Rumble Royale is a battle royale game," I explained, speaking into a translation app on my phone, which I had downloaded earlier that day during a break at school. "In solos, you start out with one hundred players, and the last player standing wins. With squads, you start with twenty-five four-player teams. Either way, we all start in this flying bus and then hop out and pick a spot on the map to start out." I clicked the "translate" button on the app, hoping it did a good job of explaining all that.

When the War Wagon got close to one of my favorite landing spots, my avatar jumped out and flew down on my glider. The moment Shu saw my glider, her face lit up.

"Dragon!" she said, pointing at the screen.

"That's right," I replied, asking why she knew that word and why she was so excited about it. She took a moment to explain the importance of the Chinese dragon dance and showed me a picture of the huge dragon puppets Chinese people use in parades, often with several people inside making them move. They were pretty cool. She also told me that the year 2024 happened to be the year of the dragon on the Chinese zodiac, which was supposed to bring luck, wealth, and power. Considering what I was trying to pull off, I liked the sound of that.

"It's called the Royal Dragon glider," I explained, drawing her attention back to the game as I landed. "It's super rare. Only players who bought the season two game pass have them."

I went on to explain that my avatar's skin was pretty rare too. Called the Noir Knight, it was only available to players who bought *Rumble Royale's* first-ever game pass in chapter one, season two. To get it, players not only had to purchase the game pass but also make it to level seventy, so the number of people who owned the skin was pretty small.

"Okay, this is where things get interesting," I said, rubbing my hands together in anticipation.

- 5 -

"After you land on the map, preferably on high ground where there aren't too many other players, you have to start looting, which means gathering as many items as possible—weapons, ammo, medicine, wood, brick, metal, you name it," I explained. I had no idea how much the translation app was picking up, but I hoped Shu could figure most things out just by watching.

"To loot materials, you use your sledgehammer like this," I continued, demonstrating on screen by whacking everything in sight—walls, trees, a truck, fences, rocks. Like my skin and my glider, my sledgehammer was also ultra rare. Called the Zapper, it was only available as a game pass reward from season two, chapter one. Players had to reach level sixty-three to unlock it. It was gold with a sparking head, and it rippled with an electrical current. Not only was it rare, it looked super cool.

"You keep track of all your resources here," I said, pointing to the spot on the bottom-right corner of the screen that tallied all of my resources. "And here," I added, switching the view so I could see my inventory and switch out my weapons, healing items—a.k.a. "heals"—and other stuff.

"While you're farming, you also want to keep an eye out for 'chests.' You can listen for them too, seeing as all chests are slightly hidden and make a sound when you get close to them. They contain all sorts of goodies." I demonstrated by opening one. "Nice—a Predator Pump Shotgun. I'll take that." I scooped up some ammo for it as well, along with a Gulp Splash. "When I drink this, it raises my shields. See?" I demonstrated by doing just that. "You have to keep an eye on your shields and your health. Your shields protect you from damage.

And if your health ever hits zero, you die. Game over! Now for the fun part," I continued, seeing as I had a reasonably good gun, some ammo, and a handful of resources. "Let's find someone to fight." Normally, it's too risky to fight someone before you have a full loadout, but I wanted to jump into the action for Shu's sake. I could see she was starting to look a little bored now that she had almost finished her cinnamon bun.

After leaping, bounding, and swimming across the map, I spotted two other players embroiled in a fierce battle that involved a combination of shooting and building. The players had used wood, metal, and brick to construct elaborate bases to protect themselves as they tried to kill their opponents and steal their resources. These two players were going at it hard considering how early it was in a game, using up all their precious resources before the real battle even began. Total scrubs, in my opinion.

"See? This is how you build a base," I said, constructing a simple two-level base out of wood. I put a pyramid on top, which became transparent. "This pyramid allows me to keep an eye out for anyone who might try to sneak up on me, but hides me from view." I crouched in the pyramid and did a full 360 to demonstrate. Shu nodded, her eyes wide as she took it all in.

"Metal is the strongest material, followed by brick and then wood. Most players use wood early on and save their stronger materials for later in the game. Wood is weaker, but it's faster to build with. It takes a bit longer to build with brick and metal, but they offer better protection. Also, no matter what you build your walls out of, you can edit them like this." With the click of a button, I changed from a ramp to a wall to a floor to a pyramid, then showed her how to add a window and door to a wall.

"Once you get good at it, when you're in a battle, you can steal someone else's wall and replace it with your own. That way, you can control the wall and edit it any way you want. Plus, see how their towers are getting higher and higher?" I pointed at the two players who were still engaged in battle. "That's what you want to do in this game—get the high ground. It gives you more control over the fight."

THE STREAM TEAM

Just then an alert sounded.

"What that?" Shu asked.

"That means the safe zone is about to shift," I explained, pointing at the screen. "The safe zone is like the eye of a hurricane. It's the only place that's safe. Not only does the zone move randomly throughout the game, it also gets smaller every time it moves. If you get caught outside of the safe zone, it's only a matter of time before you die. A key part of the game is knowing how and when to rotate from one zone to the next to avoid getting killed."

"So, outside circle bad, inside circle good?" Shu asked.

"Exactly," I replied, smiling. "Also, rotating is one of the most dangerous parts of the game," I continued. "You want to rotate early so you can avoid unnecessary fights that might get you killed. If you wait too long to rotate, though, you'll be forced to run in a straight line to get to the safe zone, which makes you an easy target. If you rotate early to a good spot, such as a piece of high ground, it sets you up to pick off players who wait too long—like that guy."

Having built a small base just inside the safe zone, I opened fire on a total noob who was bounding along just ahead of the wall of chaos that was closing in.

"Cracked him!" I yelled, which meant I had just destroyed his shield. "Got him with a headshot too!"

The player threw up a wall to protect himself.

"Normally, I wouldn't do this so early in the game, but I'm going in for the kill," I said, leaping out of my base and running toward his. "Just so you can see how it works." As I ran, I saw a green cross floating in the air in front of his base.

"That means he's trying to heal himself," I said, pointing at the cross. "But I'm not going to let him get away with that."

I opened fire on his wall, obliterating it, but he threw up another one. I kept blasting through wall after wall. I knew it was only a matter of time before he ran out of resources. I just hoped I wouldn't run out of ammo first.

"Almost got him!" I said, already able to taste the kill.

Suddenly, my controller buzzed in my hands, and I realized I'd been hit.

"No! I'm being third partied!" I'd been so intent on getting the kill that I forgot to build a couple of walls to protect myself, and another player had appeared out of nowhere, taking advantage of the fact that I was distracted.

In desperation, I built a couple of walls and tried to heal myself with a med kit, just like the kid I had gone after had done. But it was too late, and before I knew it, I was dead. My avatar fell to the ground while a spawn drone appeared to teleport it back to Spawn Island to wait for the next War Wagon. Meanwhile, all the resources I had gathered were scattered around my avatar for another player to pick up.

"Dang it!" I said, throwing my controller onto my desk. Thankfully, I had a huge bright red mouse pad to cushion it.

"Sorry about that," I said, my cheeks glowing in embarrassment at losing my temper in front of Shu. I grabbed my controller to inspect it for damage, then turned to face her. "You shouldn't do that last part," I added, holding the controller out to her. "Well, now that you've seen how it's done, want to give it a try?"

She wiped the last of the cream cheese frosting from the corner of her mouth and nodded. "Looks fun."

I cringed, hoping her fingers weren't sticky but not wanting to ask her to wash her hands, and handed the controller to her. We were only a few minutes into this whole recruiting exercise, and I was already bending my gaming setup rules, if not breaking them.

Rules or no rules, I got out of my chair and motioned for Shu to sit. This was it. Time to see if phase one of my plan was about to go boom—or bust.

- 6 -

Rather than have Shu jump straight into a game, I had her spend some time in creative mode. That gave her a chance to learn how to run, walk, jump, slide, crouch, swim, build, and use weapons and heals without the pressure of having to avoid ninety-nine other players who were all determined to kill her.

Once she got the hang of which buttons did what, she was incredibly fast, especially at building and editing. In fact, within twenty minutes, I would have thought she'd been playing *Rumble Royale* for her entire life. I was just about to suggest she try out a real game and see how she performed under pressure when I heard someone come down the stairs.

"Whatcha doin'?" Olivia asked in a sing-song voice as she walked up and peered over Shu's shoulder.

"None of your business," I replied, frowning. That was pretty much my automatic response to anything Oliva asked. She wasn't a bad sister, if I was being completely honest about it, but she was way too nosy for her own good.

"Wow, she's fast." Olivia watched Shu's lightning-speed builds and edits for a moment and then turned to me. "I bet she's even faster than you, Wyatt. Way faster."

"Whatever," I said. "You shouldn't even be down here." I made sure to sound grumpy, but inside, I was delighted at how well Shu was doing. And to have Olivia confirm it convinced me that it wasn't just wishful thinking on my part.

Just then, Shu set the controller down and looked at her watch. When she did, her eyebrows shot up, and she leaped to her feet, shoving my gaming chair back so fast that Olivia and I had to leap out of the way.

"What's wrong?" I asked as I stared at her in alarm, wondering if something in the game had spooked or offended her. I was fast realizing that I knew next to nothing about Chinese culture, something I would have to spend some time Googling later.

"Curfew," Shu said, pointing at her watch. "Have to go."

"Already?" I looked at the clock on my computer monitor, which showed it was only 4:45 p.m.

"Have to get home by five o'clock or big trouble. Host parents very strict."

On her way out, Shu paused and touched her lips, then rubbed her belly, smiling at Olivia. "Mmm . . . good," she said. "Thank you!"

Olivia grinned at her. "Anytime, Shu. Now 'shoo' before you get into trouble!"

After walking Shu to the door and promising to meet up with her at school the next day to talk more about her joining my team, I returned to my gaming room and plunked down in my chair. Only then did I remember my untouched cinnamon bun—

and my growling stomach. Deciding I had almost broken my "no food or drink" rule near my gaming setup already—I had a good reason to celebrate, after all—I took a huge bite and then stared up at the RPG lights on my ceiling, which were slowly morphing through a rainbow of colors. As I chewed, my mouth bursting with a delicious mixture of sugar and cinnamon, I couldn't help but smile. Shu might be a girl, an exchange student from China with strict host parents, not much English, and only a short time left to stay in our country, but I could already tell she was a *Rumble Royale* champion in the making, and I was determined to ride her coattails all the way to the top.

Phase one of my plan was complete. Now that I had speed and reflexes, it was time to find the next member of my squad, and I knew just the place to look.

- 7 -

Danger: Nerd Alert!!

That was what a handwritten sign taped on the door to my next destination said in bright red letters against a black background.

Even though being called a nerd used to be a negative thing—a word that my parents used *way* back in the day to describe someone who was unstylish or socially awkward—these days, being a nerd is cool. All it means is someone who's obsessed with a TV series, a movie franchise, or in my case, a video game.

I wasn't looking for just any kind of nerd to be

the second member of my crack *Rumble Royale* squad, though. I was looking for a special type of nerd. A nerd among nerds, you might say. Someone who was so smart and so obsessive that once they were on the hunt, there was no stopping them.

Why was I looking for a nerd? To fill out the next two items on my list of champion video game player qualities—top notch problem-solving skills and a desire to win at any cost.

You see, there are a couple of things about nerds you may not know. First of all, nerds are way smarter than the average person. Plus, nerds aren't merely fans of the things they enjoy. They're more like fanatics. They don't just love the objects of their obsession—they know everything about them, endlessly discussing and dissecting them until there's nothing left but a pile of crumbs on the floor. But heaven help any noob who dares to do the same, or even worse, if the studio, the creator, or the company responsible for the thing they love changes it in some small and seemingly insignificant way. Nerds go ballistic about stuff like that. Total flame war.

players win or lose based on skill and strategic decision making, not luck.

There was one player in particular I wanted to approach: Lucas Maxwell. He was tall and gangly, with a mass of curly hair that was perpetually tangled and unwashed—rumor had it he was doing a top-secret, government-funded long-term hair grease accumulation test. He also had a tendency to wear sweatpants that were way too short paired with a T-shirt featuring one of his favorite obscure heavy metal bands, all of which made him look like the furthest thing from a future *Rumble Royale* champion that a person could get. But when it came to *Warhammer*, Lucas was undefeated. He was such a fanatic about it that he claimed he had developed an algorithm that would allow him to win virtually any scenario. I can't even tell you what an algorithm is—I've never been too good at math—but from what I'd heard, it seemed to be working flawlessly.

The thing is, even though people like Lucas are masters at strategy games, they don't exactly win any awards when it comes to social skills. Maybe

THE STREAM TEAM

That brings me to the second reason why I wanted a nerd on my *Rumble Royale* squad. Not only are they smart and obsessive, which helps with the strategy part, they're also super competitive. There's nothing a nerd loves more than flexing on other nerds, and there's nothing a nerd hates more than another nerd knowing—or at least claiming to know—more than they do. Or even worse, having a different opinion, especially if they can't back it up. I've almost seen fistfights break out over arguments like who's the best actor ever to play Spider-Man—Tobey Maguire, Andrew Garfield, or Tom Holland—or what's the coolest skin in *Call of Duty*. Someone who was willing to go down swinging over such seemingly trivial things was *exactly* the type of person I was looking for. And what better place to find such a person than our school's tabletop gaming club?

Don't get me wrong. These guys—and a handful of girls—didn't play tabletop games like *Monopoly* or *Risk*. I'm talking about *Dungeons & Dragons, Magic: The Gathering,* and the grandmaster of them all, *Warhammer*—games where

THE STREAM TEAM

because they've been rejected so often as weird or different, they aren't the most welcoming group. They're often suspicious of outsiders, assuming that whenever anyone outside their little group approaches them, they're being set up to be mocked or ridiculed. I knew I would have to play my cards carefully, so to speak, especially since I didn't know the first thing about *Warhammer* or any other tabletop strategy games. I felt a little better about it, having brought Shu along as backup, but I probably should have done some more research first. Now that we were already in the room, though, it was way too late for that.

"I'm going to advance my Deff Dread," was the first thing I heard Lucas say as I approached. He and several other guys were huddled around a miniature version of some medieval ruins. Scattered throughout were squads of hand-painted figurines. Some of them looked like orcs dressed in spacesuits, and others looked like skeletons with huge blaster rifles. Lucas's Deff Dread was part of his orc army. It was way bigger than the rest of the figurines. It had purple armor, huge claws, and a nasty-looking flamethrower.

KEVIN MILLER

THE STREAM TEAM

Lucas rolled a die, which landed on a four. Then he pulled out a measuring tape, measured ten inches across the table, and moved his Deff Dread to that spot, well ahead of the rest of his orc army and not far from the skeleton army.

"Okay, now my orkboy's going to fire his big shoota," he said.

"Ooh, I'm shaking in my skeletal boots," the master of the skeleton army said. I'd never met him before, but I knew his name was Owen Blackmore. He had thick glasses and long blond hair parted down the middle. His stained white T-shirt said, *Never trust an atom. They make up everything.* Nerd humor, I guess. "Your orkboy's a five up," Owen said. "It couldn't hit a barn door with a banana if it was standing three feet away from it."

The other players chuckled and murmured in agreement.

"We'll see about that," Lucas replied, picking up three dice and shaking them in his hands. He rolled the dice into a black velvet-lined tray in front of him, getting a five, a six, and a one. "Two out of three ain't bad!"

"Just because you hit them doesn't mean you hurt them," Owen replied. "You need a three plus."

Lucas scooped up two of the dice and rerolled them, this time getting a four and a five. "Nice!" he said. "Two for two."

"You're forgetting that my necrons have a four-plus save," Owen said.

Don't worry if you have no idea what they're talking about. Neither did I.

"And you're forgetting what a crummy roller you are," Lucas replied, grinning.

"We'll see about that." Owen grabbed two dice, stood up, and shook them so hard, I thought they would turn into butter. When he finally let them loose into his rolling tray, everyone stood up to see the results.

"Snake eyes!" Lucas exclaimed.

"Dang it!" Owen cried. "Initiating reanimation protocol."

Lucas crossed his arms, a smug smile on his face. "Be my guest. But unless you roll fives or sixes, because of my Deff Dread's proximity to your army, it's bye-bye baby to your entire battalion, which will die in the ensuing blast."

"I'm willing to risk it," Owen replied.

"Are you sure?" Lucas asked. I had a sneaking suspicion that he was about to prove the superiority of his algorithm once again.

"Yes!" Owen said, looking as if he was about to burst.

This time he shook the dice so hard and for so long, I thought there would be nothing left but dust. Despite all the buildup, when he finally threw them into his tray, they came up as a three and a two.

"Kaboom!" Lucas mimicked an explosion and then toppled Owen's skeleton army, scattering them throughout the ruins. "Better luck next time," he said, grinning.

"Whatever," Owen muttered, scooping up his dice and then gathering the remains of his dead necron army.

The other players also stood up and did the same with their miniature figurines.

"Hey, where's everyone going?" Lucas asked. "You can't just leave in the middle of a game!"

"Your army's way too OP," one of the guys said

on his way toward the door.

"Yeah," another player echoed.

"It's not my fault he fell right into my trap after I advanced my Deff Dread! I even tried to warn him!" When Lucas got no response, he flopped down into his chair. "What a bunch of chickens," he grumbled as the other players filtered out.

Only then did Lucas notice Shu and me standing there. He looked around the otherwise empty room and then frowned as his gaze returned to us. "What do you want?"

I looked around the room too, partly out of nervousness—Lucas was a couple of years older than me and way taller, and I didn't want to tick him off—and partly to make sure no one else was listening.

"I . . . uh . . . I wanted to talk to you about joining my team," I said.

"Oh, yeah? What kind of team?" he asked as he crossed his arms over his chest, a sure sign of defensiveness. "And what kind of game?" he added, his eyes turning to slits.

To my surprise—not to mention my disappointment—Lucas's first reaction to my proposal was laughter, followed by ridicule.

"Rumble Royale? Are you serious? Isn't that game for babies?"

Shu's brow furrowed as she looked at me for an answer. I wasn't sure if she felt I had tricked her into playing a game for little kids, or if she was genuinely confused by Lucas's question.

"No, not at all," I said. "I mean, the graphics look kind of cartoonish, but Rumble Royale is all about hunting and killing your enemies and trying to be the last one standing at the end of an epic battle royale. And it's not just about shooting. It also involves all sorts of strategy in terms of the weapons you use, how you gather and use your resources, how you rotate when the safe zone shifts, and where and how you build. In fact, it's a lot like Warhammer, D and D, Magic, and all the other games you guys play here." I gestured to indicate the rest of the room, which was crammed with tables and shelves piled high with dozens of game boxes.

"I don't know," Lucas said, swiveling back and forth in his chair. "I've never really been a video game guy."

"Plus, you can win money," I said, trying to sweeten the pot. To my surprise, considering how reluctant he had been up to then, Lucas's ears perked up at the sound of that. Then I realized that buying all those Warhammer figurines and dioramas probably wasn't cheap. And come to think of it, I had never heard of a professional Warhammer player either, so maybe there weren't any chances to win money playing that game.

THE STREAM TEAM

"What kind of money?" Lucas asked, uncrossing his arms and leaning forward in his chair.

I swallowed hard as I pondered how to respond to his question. I didn't want to set the bar too low, fearing he would think it was a waste of time, but I didn't want to sound too unrealistic either by promising him the moon. I decided to aim for the middle. "Well, for starters, if you enter the free online tournaments, you can win anywhere from a hundred dollars to a thousand dollars. But if you make it all the way to the Rumble Cup, first prize is three million dollars. And the winnings for the runners up aren't too shabby either."

Lucas leaned back in his chair and scoffed. "Three million dollars? For playing some lame video game?"

I nodded in reply. Everything in me wanted to point out that I didn't think playing *Rumble Royale*—or any other video game, for that matter—was any lamer than spending all his time huddled in a dark room with a bunch of other sweaty guys painting little figurines and then pitting them against each other in mock battles. Talk about a game for babies! But I didn't want to press my luck, especially since I could feel him nibbling at the bait.

"That's right," I said. "Look at this." I pulled out my phone and brought up the site for the 2024 Rumble Royale Champions Series so he could see for himself. "Believe it or not, the prize money is more than the winners get at Wimbledon, the Indy 500, and the Masters Tournament."

As Lucas snatched my phone out of my hand and read it, I could have sworn I saw dollar signs flashing in his eyes. A moment later, he tossed my phone back to me and sat up straight for what could have been the first time in years, considering his perpetually hunched posture.

"When's the Rumble Cup?" he asked as if his mind had leaped past all the blood, sweat, and tears it would take us to get there, and he was already picturing himself standing on top of the winner's podium. Somehow I also got the feeling he pictured himself standing there alone, or worse, on top of a pile of bodies—ours included—but my imagination has always been a bit on

THE STREAM TEAM

the overactive side.

"It's not until late July, but we have a lot to do before we get there. We have to rank up and then qualify by playing in all sorts of—"

Lucas leaped to his feet, causing me and Shu to stumble back in surprise. "I don't care what it takes to get there," he said, already on his way to the door. "If there's even a slight chance of winning three million dollars playing some lame video game—"

I winced at his use of that term again.

"I'll figure out how to do it."

Before we knew it, the door had slammed shut behind him. Shu and I looked at each other in confusion. Then she typed something into her cell phone and held it up for me to see.

"'What now?'" I said, reading the translation aloud. "Good question." It sounded like Lucas had just agreed to join our squad, but why had he walked out on us? Was he planning to go off and start his own team? I kicked myself for giving him the idea. The last thing we needed were even more competitors, especially smart ones like him.

Before I had a chance to kick myself again, the

door flew open, and Lucas stuck his head back inside the room. "Well, don't just stand there like a couple of twits. Show me how to play this game!"

When the door slammed behind him yet again, I looked over at Shu, and we shared a grin. I'm not sure if she realized it or not, but this time Lucas had left out the word "lame."

Maybe this was going to be easier than I thought.

- 9 -

Then again, maybe not.

As I was about to learn, when it came to Lucas Maxwell, nothing was easy. Instead, he had a tendency to complicate everything. First item on the list?

Finances.

"For starters, I want fifty percent of whatever we win," he said.

"Fifty percent?" I replied, my jaw dangling open. "But there are four members on the team—at least, there will be soon—so it's only fair if we split our winnings four ways."

I couldn't believe he was already talking about money. After all, even though I had managed to convince Lucas to check out the game, he still hadn't spent even one second playing it. I had no idea if he even *could* play, never mind if he was any good, so there was no way I was going to agree to turn over half of our winnings to him right out of the gate.

Before I realized what was happening, Lucas stood up out of my gaming chair, sending it rolling across the room, and headed for the stairs.

"Wait. Where are you going?" I asked, casting a helpless glance at Shu. Judging by the look of fear and confusion in her eyes, I realized she probably had no idea what was going on either.

"Where do you think? To start my own team," Lucas replied, not even bothering to look back.

"Wait a second," I said, the firmness in my tone causing Lucas to stop in his tracks. My gaze bounced back and forth between him and Shu as my brain raced to find a way to keep Lucas from going up those stairs and making one of my worst fears come true.

THE STREAM TEAM

"I can give you thirty percent," I blurted, deciding on the spot to take the extra five percent out of my share. The thought of us winning *anything* still seemed like an impossible dream at that point, so what did it matter if I agreed to give him an extra five percent of nothing? And if that's what it took to make my dream come true and avoid becoming a nine-to-five drone in an office park somewhere in the suburbs when I grew up, so be it. I just hoped I wouldn't live to regret my decision.

To my surprise, Lucas broke into a grin. Then he turned around and came back toward me, his hand thrust out. "That wasn't so hard, was it? We can shake on it now and write up a contract later. You'll be our witness, right, Shu?" He looked at her for a response. I doubted she knew what he had just said, so when she glanced at me, I nodded, and she repeated the gesture, nodding at Lucas, a big smile on her face.

"Deal," Lucas said, gripping my hand and squeezing it so hard, I yelped in pain.

"Hey, easy on the merchandise!" I said, yanking my arm away. "How do you expect me to play with a broken hand?"

"Probably no worse than you do right now," Lucas said, snickering.

This guy was something else. He didn't know the first thing about *Rumble Royale,* and he was already criticizing my play? Who did he think he was?

Lucas grabbed my gaming chair from where it had bumped up against the wall and rolled it back in front of my monitors. "Okay, let's do this," he said, stretching his arms out in front of him and cracking his knuckles before picking up my controller. "Where do we begin?"

- 10 -

Lucas's first walk-through didn't go nearly as smoothly as Shu's. For one thing, he was a terrible listener, and he wouldn't let me show him anything. Instead, he wanted to do everything himself. Each time I reached out for the controller to demonstrate something, he yanked it away.

"Just tell me which buttons to push and in what order," he said. I let out a big sigh and then did just that. "And forget creative mode," he added. "I want to try this out for real."

"But you hardly even know how to move around the map," I protested, "never mind how

to build or fight."

"Yeah, well, there's no better way to learn than to jump right in," he replied.

I could think of a few better ways to learn, one of which was doing exactly what I told him, but I could already tell that arguing with Lucas Maxwell was a waste of time.

As I predicted, his first game went terribly. Not only did he leave the War Wagon way earlier than he should have, he headed straight for Tipsy Towers, the same spot as practically everyone else. With so many other players crowded into such a small area, he had barely gotten his hands on a gun—a junky one at that—before someone killed him. He hadn't even looted a single resource.

"How do I get back to the lobby?" he asked.

"Here, I'll show you," I replied, reaching for the controller, but once again, he yanked it away.

"Just tell me."

Heaving out a huge sigh of annoyance, I did just that, and before I knew it, he was back on the War Wagon, flying high above the map yet again.

"This time maybe wait a little longer to—" Before I had a chance to complete my sentence, he was already airborne and on his glider. "Or just jump out along with everyone else," I muttered, assuming I was about to witness a repeat of his first failed attempt to survive more than a few seconds.

This time when he landed, however, instead of racing into a building to grab a gun like everyone else, he ran and crouched in a bush.

"What are you doing?" I asked. "All the best weapons are going to get taken."

"Maybe, but racing for a gun was how I got

killed last time. This is a battle royale, right?" Lucas turned his avatar as he watched the other players run past him, some of them already firing at one another. Because he was in a bush, no one could see him. Besides, no one would think anyone would be bored enough to try something like that straight away. I was going to point that out to Lucas, but I wanted to avoid another pointless argument, so I decided against it.

"Yes," I said, unsure where his question was leading.

"So, the goal of the game isn't to hunt and kill your enemies like you told me when we first met. It's to survive until the end of the game, to be the last player standing, right?"

"Yeah. Or the last duo or squad standing if you're part of a team. But kills can—"

"I get it. You earn points for kills and points for surviving, and if you kill someone, you can take their resources, but if you look at the risk-reward ratio, it doesn't make sense to get involved in a fight until you absolutely have to, right? Especially because you have no idea who you're going

THE STREAM TEAM

up against. They could be the worst player in the game, but they could be the best."

I let out a puff of air, knowing he was right but not wanting to admit it. Plus, I loved getting into fights, which may have been one reason why I was struggling so much to win. I mean, what was the point of gathering up all those cool guns and ammo if you weren't going to use them?

"Yeah, but—"

"It makes way more sense to spend the first part of the game gathering resources, stockpiling weapons, ammo, heals, and shields while building, moving, and fighting as little as possible so other players don't notice you, right?"

I couldn't believe Lucas had figured all that out after playing the game for only a few minutes.

My shoulders slumped even lower than before. "Yeah."

"So, that's why I'm hiding in this bush. It's silent, it doesn't require any resources, and once everyone has moved on, then I'll start looting."

"But what if no good weapons are left?" I protested.

"I don't need a *good* weapon," Lucas replied, already moving his avatar out of the bush. "I just need *a* weapon. Correction—I need *three* weapons. One for long range, one for medium range, and one for close-range fighting. Am I right?"

"Yeah," I replied, yet again amazed at how quickly he was figuring things out. "You also need ammo," I added, hoping to point out at least one thing he hadn't thought of yet. "And if you're smart, you'll also want to upgrade your weapons. To do that, you need—"

"You don't think I'm smart? Isn't that why you recruited me?" Lucas asked. A grin stole onto his face as he used his sledgehammer to loot metal from a semi-trailer that no one else had bothered to loot. "Well, will you look at that?" he said as he came across an untouched chest hidden inside the trailer. Each chest in *Rumble Royale* contains a random combination of weapons, ammo, heals, and resources such as wood, stone, metal, and gold bars. The gold bars are what players use to upgrade their guns, as I had just tried to explain to Lucas. Once he opened the chest, to my surprise, out

THE STREAM TEAM

popped a Gulp Splash, some random resources, and a sick-looking weapon.

"A Saber Tooth Shotgun?" I exclaimed. "That's one of the best guns in the game!"

"Looks like it came with ammo, too," Lucas said, scooping it up.

I shook my head in disbelief. Talk about beginner's luck.

But as I continued to watch Lucas navigate around the map, I realized luck didn't have much to do with it. Even though it was Lucas's first real game—not counting the one where he died right away—his quick mind enabled him to figure out the best strategy in almost every situation, from looting to building to rotating. He didn't get in a fight until only nine other players were left, and he only lost because he'd never gotten in a fight before, and he was terrible at aiming, never mind shooting and building, but once he figured out which buttons did what . . .

"You need a better controller," he said, tossing it onto my desk as his avatar collapsed to the ground and his impressive collection of resources scattered around it.

"Hey, take it easy with that thing!" I said, casting a glance at Shu, who had seen me do the same thing with the controller a couple of days earlier. I didn't want her to start thinking it was acceptable behavior.

"What do you mean, I need a better controller?" I asked, snatching it up and inspecting it for damage. "Just because you can't shoot straight doesn't mean there's something wrong with my controller."

Lucas snickered, then offered a one-shoulder shrug. "Whatever you say, boss. I just know that when I set up *my* gaming rig, there's no way I'm using one of those things."

All I could do was shake my head in exasperation. One of "those things" just happened to be the best controller on the market. Lucas had spent ten minutes playing the game, and he already considered himself an expert on the hardware too? That reminded me of another quality that all nerds share apart from intelligence and competitiveness—arrogance. Hopefully, that quality wouldn't overshadow the other two.

Speaking of negative qualities, Olivia chose

that moment to come down the stairs and butt in on our gaming sesh.

"Whatcha doin'?" she asked in her typical fashion as she sauntered into the room, as if she didn't know. When she saw Lucas, she stopped and stared. "*Two* friends? You brought two friends home? I didn't know you had any friends, Wyatt, never mind *two*."

Lucas grinned. "Who's she supposed to be, the fourth member of our squad?" He looked her up and down, noting her miniature size. "Correction—the third-and-a-half member?"

Olivia put her hands on her hips and glared at him. "Look who's talking, Mr. Wacky Wavy Inflatable Arm-Flailing Tube Man. As for joining your team, that'll be the day. I wouldn't be caught dead playing some buffle-headed video game, least of all with a string bean like you!"

Lucas's grin widened, then he swiveled in his chair to face me. "Buffle-headed? I like this girl. What did you say her name was?"

"I'm right here, you know," Olivia said, her annoyance growing. "You can talk *to* me, not *about* me."

"Her name's Olivia, and no, she's not the fourth member of our squad. She's my little sister, and she was just leaving. Right, Olivia?"

As I glared at her to make sure my words sank in, her angry face transformed into a smile, and she looked past me and waved. I glanced over my shoulder and saw Shu smiling at her as she waved back.

"Actually, I was just about to leave, Wyatt, if you must know, and I'm taking Shu with me."

She stepped forward and grabbed Shu's hand, pulling her toward the stairs.

"Wait. You can't take Shu," I protested. "She's part of our team. We need to talk about strategy!" I gave Shu a pleading look, but she just smiled and shrugged as if she had no choice in the matter.

"Too late, BattleBot. I already booked a session with her."

"A session? Doing what?" I asked, watching dumbfounded as Olivia led Shu up the stairs.

"Her nails, duh."

"But how did you book it?"

"On Snapchat. How do you think?"

With that, they were gone. I shook my head in

disbelief. Olivia had already added Shu on Snapchat? I hadn't even done that yet.

I turned back to Lucas and shrugged in defeat. "I guess it's just you and me," I said, suddenly missing Shu's silent presence more than ever. I had never been alone with Lucas before, and I realized I had no idea how to engage with him one on one.

"Correction," Lucas said as he rose to his feet and clapped his paddle-like hand on my shoulder. "It's just you."

"But you can't leave yet," I protested as he headed for the stairs. "We've hardly gotten started."

"I've seen enough," Lucas replied. "Just let me know when you find the fourth member of our squad." He paused partway up the stairs. "And don't forget—thirty percent. I'm holding you to it!"

With that, he bounded up the stairs, his rangy legs allowing him to take the steps three at a time. "And no need to see me to the door. I can find my own way out!"

Thankful to be let off the hook, I sank into my gaming chair and huffed in frustration, wondering if Lucas was going to be more trouble than he was worth. Then again, he was right about one thing—it was time to seek out the fourth member of our squad. I just hoped he wouldn't be as irritating as Lucas.

Then again, who could be?

- 11 -

"Ohm . . . Ohm . . . Ohm . . ."

Less than twenty-four hours after Lucas's training session, I was back on my mission to recruit the world's greatest *Rumble Royale* squad. This time, instead of a room full of sweaty tabletop gaming nerds or a gym full of table tennis wannabes, I was sitting cross-legged on a yoga mat at the back of a room full of other students who were doing the same, as soft instrumental music played in the background.

Actually, the other students weren't cross-legged. They were in something called the lotus position, which meant instead of their feet resting on the floor *under* their legs like mine were, somehow they had managed to cross their legs and get their feet up on *top* of their thighs. However, the backs of my hands were resting on my knees, just like theirs, my thumbs and forefingers forming circles as if I was saying everything was "A-OK," and my eyes were closed. I was also chanting in time with the rest of the group, which explains the "Ohm..." thing. Supposedly, chanting like that would align our breathing with our minds so we could enter an elevated state of consciousness, whatever that was.

I guess this is a good time to tell you where I was—in a meditation session run by our school's mindfulness club, the Medi-Taters. In case you're wondering, yes, that's a play on words, and yes, their logo was an actual "tater," also known as a potato. They even had this mindfulness segment called "Tater Thoughts " that they would do as part of the announcements over the intercom each morning. I know, real "punny." I would have given anything for an actual tater tot at that moment. I was just thankful that the noise of our chanting drowned out the sound of my grumbling stomach—at least I thought it did.

"Shh . . ." a voice beside me hissed.

I opened one eye and glared at the person to my right. My gaze was met by one of the worst cases of bedhead I had ever seen. It was accompanied by an Animals as Leaders T-shirt with the neck so stretched, it looked like it had been washed about a thousand times. Plus, his lotus position was causing his already-too-short sweatpants to ride up even farther than normal on his hairy legs. I was amazed that someone with such long legs could even bend them into that position. He looked like a human pretzel.

In case you're wondering who I'm talking about, yes, it was Lucas. Even though he had told me to let him know when I found the next member of our squad, once I revealed where I was going to recruit that person, Lucas had insisted on coming with me. I suppose it was his way of supervising the deal, making sure I didn't renege on the thirty percent of our winnings that I'd promised him—or, worse yet, offer an even better deal to someone else. Either that or maybe he just didn't believe I could pull it off on my own. But I had already managed to recruit Lucas and Shu, so why wouldn't I be able to do this?

As we continued to chant, I peeked at the other students. They all seemed to be right into it, although I still couldn't figure out why. I mean, sure, it's probably a good idea to take some time each day to clear your head and all, to refocus on what's most important and eliminate stress, but to join a club where that's all you do? These kids could be doing any number of things, from football to basketball to soccer to lacrosse, but instead they were sitting in that room trying to achieve inner peace or something. What can I say? To each his own.

The person I was interested in just happened to be the fifteen-year-old African American kid who was leading the session, although the way he carried himself, he seemed much older than that. His name was Darian. Sitting up front in a perfect lotus position with a calm expression on his face, he looked like the embodiment of "inner peace"— not to mention the exact *opposite* of a hothead

THE STREAM TEAM

like Lucas. But that was precisely why I wanted to recruit Darian to our squad. He was the kind of guy we all needed to help us keep calm under pressure—a quality I felt I needed more and more the longer I hung around with Lucas.

"Psst..."

I glared at Lucas, then glanced around to make sure no one else was paying attention.

"What?" I whispered.

"If Darian's so deep into this touchy-feely, soul-searching gobbledygook, do you think he even knows what video games are?"

"Of course he does," I hissed, conscious that some of the other students were shooting dirty looks at us. "Everyone knows what video games are."

"But does he know how to play them?"

"I don't know. But he can learn. Just like you—and Shu."

"Shh..."

That came from Shu herself, who was sitting on the other side of me. Once Lucas said he was coming to the meditation session, she decided to tag along too.

"With our luck, he's probably a vegetarian or something and is philosophically opposed to violence of all kinds," Lucas said, undeterred by Shu's shush, "especially violent video games."

"Shh!"

That came from several people at once, accompanied by scowls. All three of us closed our eyes again, and I tried to settle in, but Lucas's last comment worried me. He was right. *Rumble Royale* was all about shooting and surviving until the end.

Would that go against Darian's basic programming? I certainly hoped not. But no matter how many times I said "Ohm" after that, inner peace seemed to slip further and further away—and my fear of actually having to work for a living grew bigger and bigger.

- 12 -

Lucas was wrong about one thing at least: Darian wasn't a vegetarian; he was a vegan. I was afraid that would turn out to be even worse.

"I'm actually a 'level five vegan,'" Darian explained, once we pulled him aside after the session. "That means I don't eat anything that casts a shadow." When he saw the horrified looks on our faces, Darian broke into a grin and elbowed me in the ribs. "I'm kidding! I'm just a normal vegan. But think about it: if everyone switched to a purely plant-based diet, imagine all the needless suffering we'd be able to alleviate, not to mention the millions of animals we'd be able to save."

"Um, I think you're forgetting something," Lucas said. "The only reason those animals are alive at all is because we grow them for food. So, are you saying it would be better if the millions of cows, chickens, and pigs that get turned into burgers, nuggets, and sausages each year at McDonald's never lived at all?"

That question seemed to catch Darian flat-footed, as if he'd never considered it before, but only for a moment. "Did you know pigs are as smart as dogs?" he asked, shifting the direction of the argument. "How would you feel if you were driving down the highway one day, and instead of a semi-truck full of terrified pigs on their way to the slaughterhouse, it was full of labradoodles, French bulldogs, golden retrievers, and chihuahuas?"

"For starters, chihuahuas are yappy, bug-eyed little dogs," Lucas replied. "As for labradoodles—"

"Chihuahuas may be yappy, but would you want a chihuahua burger as part of your Happy Meal?"

"Um, I think we're getting a little off track here," I said, stepping between them as I forced a smile.

"Let's start over. My name is Wyatt, and these are my friends, Lucas and Shu. Shu's from China, by the way, so she doesn't speak much—"

Before I could continue, Darian stuck his hand toward Shu and spoke to her in a language I didn't understand. Apparently, she did understand it, though, because she smiled in surprise, shook his hand, then replied to him in what sounded like the same language, only she spoke it much quicker and with a different accent than he did.

"You . . . you speak Chinese?" I asked, staring at Darian in shock. He shrugged.

"Enough to get by. And it's *Mandarin*, by the way, not Chinese. There are about ten times as many Mandarin speakers in the world as there are Cantonese speakers—Cantonese is the other major Chinese language. Plus, all the best 'mindfulness books' were originally written in Mandarin, so I figured it was worth a shot."

"Wow, so you really are into this stuff," I said, my mind reeling in response to this revelation. If Darian was *that* into this mindfulness thing, I was certain there was no way he would ever consider our proposition.

"I guess you could say that," he replied. "So, what was it you guys wanted to talk to me about?"

I looked at Lucas and then at Shu—and then an idea struck me. "You know what? Why don't I let *her* tell you?" I nodded to Shu. When she tilted her head to the side in confusion, I pointed at Darian. "The game. Tell him about the game."

Her eyes lit up. "Oh, the game. Yes!"

As she launched into an explanation in Mandarin—speaking slowly, so Darian could understand her—I crossed my arms in satisfaction and looked at Lucas. For some strange reason, he didn't appear nearly as confident as I felt. A few minutes later, my expression began to mirror Lucas's when, instead of smiling and agreeing to join our team, Darian scooped up his yoga mat, rolled it up, and headed for the door as if he was horribly offended.

"Hey, wait a second. Where are you going?" I asked, following him. I glanced back at Shu in alarm. "Shu, what did you say to him?" She just threw her arms up in confusion.

"She told me enough," Darian said as he reached

the door. His hand on the doorknob, he turned back and looked at us. "I can't believe you came in here and disrupted my mindfulness session with your whispering—yes, I heard you all the way up front, as did everyone else—just so you could pitch me on playing some violent video game."

"But no animals are killed in Rumble Royale," I pointed out, hoping that might appeal to his vegan nature. "Only people." Hearing myself say it out loud made me realize that actually sounded worse.

"Correction," Lucas said, holding up his index figure. "That's not completely true. There's this llama that wanders around, and if you shoot it enough times, it gives you stuff. You can also go fishing, and whenever you eat a fish, it boosts your health."

"Lucas..." I growled. He wasn't making things any easier. I didn't know how he knew all that seeing as he had only played the game for a few minutes, but at least it told me that he was doing his homework.

"I don't care if the game is about killing people or animals," Darian said. "Killing is killing, and it's all terrible."

THE STREAM TEAM

"The game is more about surviving than killing," I said, my voice weakening as I sensed defeat bearing down on us, but I wasn't about to give up yet. "Players actually go out of their way to avoid fights for as long as possible. Isn't that right, Lucas?" I turned to him for support, but before he could reply, Darian did.

"You don't get it," Darian said. "Killing, surviving—it doesn't matter. The game is still teaching you that this is a dog-eat-dog world. Survival of the fittest. Kill or be killed. No wonder the real world is getting more and more violent with millions of kids like you spending hours doing stuff like that."

He opened the door, about to storm out.

"Actually," Lucas said, his voice freezing Darian in his tracks, "for starters, the world isn't getting more violent. In fact, statistics show that things are moving in the opposite direction. No matter which category you look at, violence has been declining worldwide for decades, even centuries. You may not believe me, but I can show you the data. I did a research paper on it for my social studies class last semester.

"As for video games leading to real-world violence, arrests for violent crime in the US have decreased steadily since the early 1990s in children, teens, and adults, and this decrease has coincided with a rapid increase in the number of video games and their popularity. Over the past twenty years alone, we've seen an over eighty-percent reduction in youth violence in North America alone. Meanwhile, sales of video games—including so-called 'violent' video games like Rumble Royale—have gone through the roof. And if you don't believe me, I can show you..."

As Lucas prattled on about how he could prove what he was saying, not only was Darian staring at him in amazement, so was I. How had Lucas managed to pull all that out of his back pocket at a moment's notice? And was *Lucas,* the world's biggest naysayer, really going to be the one to help save my dream?

"I'm smart, remember?" Lucas said when he was finished, as if answering my unspoken question. "I do my research. You don't think I would have committed to this thing if I thought it was going to turn me into a psychopath, do you?"

I shook my head. "No, but I didn't think—"

I paused when Shu said something to Darian in Mandarin. As she spoke, she raised her hands above her head, palms out, then closed her eyes and exhaled through her mouth as she lowered them, as if calming herself. Darian nodded in understanding as he watched her. Lucas and I also stared at her until she completed the motion and opened her eyes, a smile bursting onto her face. Despite everything else that was going on at that moment, I realized I really liked it when she smiled.

Still staring at her, I snapped out of it long enough to realize that for some strange reason, Darian still hadn't run out on us.

"What did she say to you?" I asked.

"If I understood her correctly, she said that killing the demons in a video game calms the demons in the mind. That's why video games don't increase violence in the real world. Instead, they help reduce it by allowing players to expend all their negative energy and enter a flow state."

"A flow what?"

"A *flow state*. Also known as being 'in the zone.' A mental state in which a person is completely focused on a single task or activity—exactly the sort of state we try to achieve here as part of the Medi-Taters."

"So . . . what do you think about all that?" I asked, not wanting to push things but really wanting to hear his answer.

Rather than replying immediately, Darian stepped back into the classroom and pulled the door shut behind him.

"Tell me more about this game," he said.

Lucas and I shared a secret grin and then turned to Shu. Who would have guessed that she would be our secret weapon when it came to recruiting?

- 13 -

It might appear as if our first encounter with Darian ended well, but like most things that seem too good to be true, it was. The deal I had to make to get him on board came with all sorts of conditions.

While Darian had "kind of" committed to joining our squad, the only way he would even consider making it official was if all three of us agreed to join the Medi-Taters, at least until the end of the school year. He said from what he had observed of us so far, we could benefit from spending more time practicing mindfulness, but I think he was really just talking about Lucas.

Our first task as members of the group? Doing the following day's edition of "Tater Thoughts" on the intercom for the whole school. So, there we were—Darian, Lucas, Shu, and me—huddled around the microphone in the front office.

"What did the yoga police say to the bank robber?" I asked, reading from a script that Darian had prepared for us.

"You have the right to remain silent!" Lucas replied, grinning like a maniac. Did he actually think that joke was funny?

THE STREAM TEAM

I glanced at Principal Ewing and Mrs. Siedlecki, our school secretary, both of whom were straight-faced but motioned for us to continue. That's when I remembered we were on a hot mic, the audio piped live into every classroom.

"Um, two men meet on the street, and one asks the other . . ." I motioned for Lucas to say his part. Before he did, he cleared his throat and then deepened his voice to a ridiculously low level.

"Hi, how are you? And how's your son? Is he still unemployed?"

"Yes he is," I replied, speaking for the other man. "But he's meditating now."

"Meditating? What's that?" Lucas asked, again in his ridiculously low voice.

"I don't know," I said, "but it's sure better than him sitting around doing nothing!"

I'm not sure if either of us expected a round of applause or laughter in response to that joke or what. Darian, who had contributed the joke, seemed to think it was hilarious. All I could imagine were hundreds of kids staring at their classroom's intercom in stunned silence, wondering if we'd lost our minds rather than getting them under control.

"Okay, that does it for the humor portion of today's broadcast," Darian said, "so we'll end with a final thought. 'It's not what you look at that matters, it's what you see.' That's from Henry David Thoreau, in case any of you were wondering. And in case you don't know who that is . . ."

I hate to say it, but I think the only thing the people listening to our broadcast were wondering about was when this torture was going to end.

Once we had suitably embarrassed ourselves, it seemed like we had passed some kind of test in Darian's eyes because after school, instead of his usual level-headedness, he was jonesing to come over to my place and take a crack at *Rumble Royale*. Apparently, after talking some more with Lucas, Darian had also done his homework, and he had gone from one of the biggest critics of video games to one of their biggest fans. Seeing as he had yet to even dip his toe into Lost Lake, even I was worried he was getting ahead of himself. However, before I knew it, once again I found myself on my way home after school with not one, not two, but three friends in tow. And, sure enough, you-know-who was there to greet us at the door.

"Wow. Did you just win a popularity contest or something, Wyatt?" Olivia asked. Then she leaned in close and put one hand in front of her mouth as she lowered her voice. "Or do these people just feel really sorry for you?"

Olivia. Grrr...

"Hi, Shu. Hi, String Bean," she continued, her face brightening. Then she frowned at Darian. "Who's the third amigo?"

"I'm Darian," he said, smiling as he held out his hand for her to shake. "And you must be Olivia."

She held her free hand to her chest in mock surprise. "You already know my name? I feel so honored."

"You should actually feel terrible for wasting our time," I said. "Now, if you'll just—"

"I sure hope that's not the sound of you and your sister arguing in front of our guests, Wyatt," Mom said as she walked into the entryway, car keys jingling in her hand. "I'm Mrs. Kelsey, by the way," she added, shaking hands with Darian and

Lucas, the latter of whom she had missed meeting the last time he came over.

"It's such a pleasure to meet you," Darian said. Still holding her hand, he closed his eyes and took a deep breath through his mouth, letting it out slowly through his nose. All of us stood and stared at him, wondering what he was up to. Olivia's eyes were practically popping out of her head at his strange behavior, and even my mom looked like she was trying to stifle a giggle. When Darian finally opened his eyes, he smiled at my mom. "Your home has such a pleasant vibe, Mrs. Kelsey. It's so ... tranquil."

My mom's smile wavered. I think she was still trying not to laugh. I mean, "tranquil"? What fifteen-year-old guy uses a word like that?

"Why, thank you, Darian," Mom said as she tried not to make a big show out of extracting her hand from Darian's grasp. "What can I say? We do our best." She seized the moment to grab a light jacket and sling her purse over her shoulder. "Well, it's a pity Olivia and I have to run out or I'd get you all something to eat, but Wyatt knows his way around the kitchen. You make sure none of your friends go hungry, okay?"

"Yes, Mom," I replied, my tone indicating it would be just fine if she and Olivia would leave . . . oh, I don't know, five minutes ago.

"Aw, Mom, do I have to go?" Olivia asked. "I'd rather stay home and hang out with Shu." She shot a grin at her new best friend, who grinned right back.

"No way," I said, cutting Olivia off at the pass. "Shu's here on business. She doesn't have time to mess around doing her nails or makeup or anything like that. Isn't that right, Shu?"

I looked back at her, hoping for instant confirmation. Instead, she had a confused expression on her face, either because she had misunderstood me or she really was torn between practicing *Rumble Royale* with the rest of us or hanging out with my little sister. I hoped it was the former. Now that I finally had all four members of our squad together in my home, mere feet away from my gaming system, there was no way I was going to let anyone mess it up, least of all Olivia.

"I'm sorry, honey, but we booked this appointment weeks ago," Mom said. "But maybe we'll get back before Shu and the others have to leave."

"I sure hope so," Olivia said, rubbing her eye with her fist and pretending to pout on her way out the door. "Goodbye, Shu. Goodbye, String Bean. Goodbye . . . other guy."

"It's Darian," he said, smiling as he offered up the reminder.

"Oh, I already knew that," Olivia replied.

The truth was, Olivia was one of those people who didn't like to call anyone by their real name. She just hadn't come up with a suitable nickname for Darian yet, but I was sure she would. If not, I had a couple of suggestions for her, starting with "Captain Chill" and "Yoga Yoda." The only reason Shu got off the hook was because, to Olivia at least, Shu's name already sounded different enough to qualify as a nickname.

As for *my* nickname, I had sworn Olivia to secrecy the moment she came up with it, so there's no way I'm going to share it here.

- 14 -

By the time Mom and Olivia were out the door and I got everyone set up with food and drinks, over thirty minutes had gone by. Surprisingly, despite his strict vegan diet, Darian was easy to please, more than satisfied with raiding the fruit and vegetable drawers in our fridge. As for Lucas, rather than taking what was offered to him, he insisted on going through our pantry and cupboards until he came up with the unlikely combination of Spam, baked beans, and toast. Not only that, he also insisted on cooking them up—adding all sorts of sauces and spices in the process—and then demanding that Shu and I taste his concoction. I was beginning to realize that Lucas was the kind of person who insisted on pretty much everything. He even tried to get Darian to taste it, telling him he could use the protein, but that just led to another argument about the similarities between pigs and dogs. Thankfully, Shu was much easier to please. She was willing to eat almost anything, including Lucas's concoction. Even I had to admit that Spam and beans on toast is far better than it sounds.

That said, knowing how strict Shu's house parents were about her curfew, when Lucas's cooking extravaganza was over, I was antsy to start our training session, but as I was learning, the harder I pushed the others, especially Lucas and Darian, the slower they went.

For instance, when I finally got them all down into my gaming room, rather than diving straight into the game, Darian wanted us to do a brief meditation session first so we could all get "grounded," whatever that was. He was also obsessed with my lights, and he had me set them up so they would change in time with some meditation music he played over my speakers. I have to admit, the effect was rather soothing, but the last thing I wanted at that moment was to relax. I was ready to get hyped!

At long last, I was able to get Darian into my gaming chair so he could sample *Rumble Royale*. But even then it wasn't like we were off to the races. Unlike Lucas, who hardly wanted me to tell him anything, preferring to figure things out on his own, Darian wanted me to tell him *everything*. And not just about how to play the game, either. Even before he tried playing, he wanted to know the history of the game, how long I'd been playing it, at what points in the match I tended to lose my cool, and how playing the game made me feel overall.

How did the game make me feel? What kind of question was that? Did he think he was my counselor or something?

Not knowing how else to respond, I told him that it made me feel all sorts of things—happiness, anger, excitement. It all depended on how the game was going.

On top of that, Darian also wanted to know why winning was so important to me. "On the off chance that we actually win the championship and find ourselves the proud owners of millions of dollars, how do you think your life would change?" he asked. "What do you plan to do with your portion of the money?"

Thinking this was some kind of test, I gave him a generic answer that I thought would please him, saying I'd put some of it away for college, go on a bit of a spending spree, and also give some away to charity. When I got to that last part, Lucas erupted with scorn.

"Charity? Why would you give any of it away to charity?"

"Oh, I don't know," I replied, my voice bursting with sarcasm, "because charities help people?" I looked at Darian to back me up, which he did, offering a vigorous nod of agreement.

"That's what you think," Lucas replied. "Do your research, and you'll find that most charities have such high operating costs that they keep the bulk of the money for themselves. In fact, I saw this video on YouTube the other day that—"

"Why is winning so important to you, Lucas?"

Darian said, cutting the blabbermouth off. For a guy who was into being calm, cool, and collected, Darian could be pretty assertive when he wanted to be, and so far he was one of the few people I knew who could put Lucas in his place.

To my surprise, rather than launching into an elaborate explanation of what he'd do with the cash, waving his hands in the air as he unleashed an avalanche of arguments, Lucas clammed up, claiming his reasons for participating were classified. Remembering the dollar signs I had seen flash in his eyes when I first told him how much we could possibly win, his refusal to answer Darian only deepened the mystery. Why did Lucas need the money?

When Darian put the same question to Shu—in Mandarin, of course—she revealed that until that moment, she had no idea there was a possibility of winning any money playing *Rumble Royale*, much less millions of dollars. In fact, she had been under the impression that she would have to *pay* to play the game, which, to my surprise, she was totally willing to do. Was she that desperate for friends?

At any rate, it told me it was time to shop around for a better translation app. I even wondered if I should take Mandarin lessons or get Shu or Darian to teach me.

No one asked Darian what he planned to do with his share of any potential winnings, but he volunteered an explanation anyway. Among other things, it involved establishing a retreat center to help homeless people practice mindfulness as a way of helping them get off the street. No surprise there.

Once we got all that sorted out, it was time to walk Darian through the game. After I explained the basic dynamics of how to move, loot, build, and fight, he spent a few minutes in practice mode before Lucas insisted we get Darian into a real game. I wasn't a big fan of that idea, seeing as Darian appeared to be the weakest player on our team so far, and I wanted to put off the more violent aspects of the game for as long as possible, but what can I say? When it comes to Lucas, the word "no" doesn't have much of an effect.

As expected, Darian didn't last very long in a real game. We had him drop into a couple more

THE STREAM TEAM

games, all three of us coaching and encouraging him—me and Lucas in English and Shu in Mandarin—but he didn't do much better. Still, he didn't seem discouraged at all. Instead, he seemed excited by his repeated failures.

"'Discouragement and failure are two of the surest stepping stones to success,'" Darian said, once we finally convinced him to give it a rest. "You know who said that?" While waiting for us to answer, he repeated the saying and the question in Mandarin for Shu's benefit.

"I don't know," I replied. "You?"

"Dale Carnegie," Darian said. "Know who that is?"

I shook my head. Not only did I not know, I didn't really care either. I just wanted to get back to the game.

"The author of How to Win Friends and Influence People. It's one of the best-selling books of all time. You should give it a read, Wyatt. You too, Lucas."

"Me?" Lucas sniffed in disdain. "For starters, I don't need friends. As for influencing people, I prefer domination over influence. World domination, if possible." His face burst into an evil grin.

I rolled my eyes. That kid had spent *way* too much time playing *Warhammer*. A lesson in learning how to make friends sounded like exactly what Lucas needed. So far, it seemed like one of his greatest superpowers was driving people away from him rather than drawing them closer.

Before Darian could offer a reply to Lucas's grandiose proclamation, Shu spoke up, addressing Darian in Mandarin. After hearing what she had to say, Darian smiled and nodded. "That's so true, Shu. Thanks for sharing."

"Um, care to tell the rest of us ?" I asked.

"Oh, of course," Darian replied. "Sometimes I forget others can't understand Mandarin like I can."

A humble brag if I ever heard one.

"She was quoting Confucius."

"He's a famous Chinese philosopher," Lucas said, jumping in and speaking to me as if I was the only person in the room who didn't know who Confucius was.

"I know who Confucius is," I replied. "Everyone does." In truth, I had no idea who Confucius was, but I wasn't about to reveal that to a couple of know-it-alls like Lucas and Darian. "Which quote was it?" I asked, hoping to indicate that I knew so many quotes by Confucius that it was difficult to pick just one.

"'A person becomes great not because they have never failed, but because failure has not stopped them,'" Darian replied.

I bobbed my head in what I hoped was a sage way, pretending to ponder what he had just said.

"It means—"

"I know what it means, Lucas," I snapped, cutting him off. I turned to Shu and forced a smile. "Thanks for sharing that." Then I returned my attention to the others. "If we're finished discussing ancient Chinese philosophers, can we get back to the subject at hand? You've all had a chance to try out the game and get to know each other a bit. So, what do you say? Are you all ready to join this squad and take over the world of Rumble Royale or what?"

I put my fist in the middle, hoping the others would follow my example. Instead, no one else moved a muscle.

- 15 -

"What are you waiting for?" I asked.

Lucas looked at the others and then turned back to me. "So far we've all seen each other play, but none of us have seen *you* play—at least I haven't—so how do we know you're any good?"

I scoffed, not bothering to keep the disdain out of my voice. "*You're* questioning *my* ability to play Rumble Royale? You? Lucas Maxell?"

"Not just me. We all are. Am I right?" He cast his eyes at the other two, receiving faint nods in reply.

"Shu's seen me play," I said, turning to her for support. "Isn't that right, Shu?"

She didn't hesitate to offer a nod of agreement.

"Oh yeah? How'd he do?" Lucas asked.

"He die," she said. "Very fast."

Lucas chuckled as if that was the answer he expected.

"Only because I was trying to show you how to fight before I had a proper loadout!" I said. "Remember?"

All I got in response from her this time was a confused frown.

"It's true," I said, turning to the others. "Maybe Shu didn't quite understand it, but that's what I was doing."

"Well, there's one way to find out," Lucas said, scooping up my controller and holding it out toward me.

"What are you saying?" I asked. "You want me to audition to see if I'm good enough to join my own team?" I scoffed at the thought.

Lucas shrugged. "Something like that. I mean, we all know why you recruited *us*, but exactly what do *you* bring to the table?" He arched his brow as his eyes bore into mine, like he was trying to peer through to my soul or something.

I couldn't believe the audacity of this guy. He'd been on my team for, like, a minute, and he was already threatening to start a mutiny.

"Gimme that thing," I said, ripping the controller out of his hand.

"Wyatt, you don't have to—"

"Zip it," Lucas said, cutting Darian off.

I plopped into my gaming chair and booted up the game. Moments later, I was on the War Wagon, flying toward the map.

Driven by anger and a desire to put Lucas in his place, I threw caution to the wind, breaking every rule I had ever made for myself in the game. Instead of going for the least populated place, I landed in a hotspot that was crawling with other players. And instead of biding my time and stockpiling resources before getting into a fight, as soon as I had a gun, some ammo, a few heals, and a handful of resources, I went on a seek-and-destroy mission, lasering any kid I could see. Within five minutes I had three kills—two of which were headshots—and a boatload of loot. From there I engaged in box fight after box fight, racking up kill after kill as the number of players continued to dwindle and the zone got smaller and smaller.

"Okay, okay, we get the picture," Lucas said, glancing at his watch. "Places to go, people to see and all that."

"I'm not finished yet," I replied, determined to silence Lucas once and for all.

My rampage across the map continued until only three players were left. By then my kill count had leaped to fifteen. My thumbs and fingers were a blur on the controller as I built, jumped, ducked, shot, and leaped around the various structures that were crowding the ever-shrinking zone.

"No!" I cried as my avatar got pinned between a wall and a tree, unable to move. "The game's glitching out!"

At the last second, though, I managed to twist free, just in time to leap into the air and shoot the last remaining player in the head. Moments later, a glowing with "#1 Rumble Royale" written on it was floating on the screen.

"That was amazing!" Darian said, awestruck as

KEVIN MILLER

he stared at the screen. Shu's response was similar.

I set my controller on the desk and then swiveled my chair toward Lucas—the only opinion that mattered to me at the moment—my arms crossed and a smug grin on my face. "How do you like them apples?"

To my disappointment, rather than looking at my computer monitor, his eyes were on his phone. He had completely missed out on my victory.

"You weren't even watching?" I asked.

"I saw enough," Lucas replied.

"Oh, and now you're tweeting about it, I suppose?"

"Actually, no. I was just putting the finishing touches on this." Lucas finished typing on his phone, then it made a swooshing sound, presumably because he had just hit the "send" button. Sure enough, seconds later, my phone buzzed, as did everyone else's. When I looked at the screen, I realized he had just sent us a message with an attachment.

"It's a contract," Lucas explained. "Including a financial breakdown of how any potential winnings will be distributed among us. I based it on some legal partnership documents I found online. It'll do until we can get something more formal drawn up."

Once again, I shook my head in disbelief at this guy. Always looking out for number one.

"If you don't mind, I suggest we all sign it right now and—"

"No way," Darian said. "Only a fool would sign something without reading it first. I want my parents to look at it too."

"Okay, how about we take forty-eight hours to

read it and then suggest any amendments, if necessary?" Lucas said, to which the rest of us agreed.

"One more thing," I said. "Before you leave, there's something else I want to discuss."

"Oh, yeah? What's that?" Lucas asked, his hackles up. Smart, competitive, arrogant, and suspicious . . . The list of words I was using in my head to describe him was growing longer all the time, most of them not very good.

"A team name," I said. "It's not necessary to have one starting out, but I thought it would be kind of cool, and we'll definitely need one to enter tournaments. Plus, seeing as we plan on streaming our progress and creating merch and stuff, it would be smart to figure out our branding sooner rather than later."

"Good point," Lucas said, the wheels in his head already churning, which tended to happen whenever the subject of money came up.

"How about the Gamers' Guild?" I said, thinking it would be a slam dunk with Lucas considering his background in tabletop RPG games.

Lucas frowned. "Sounds like a bunch of D and D

noobs. No way."

"But I thought you were into games like D and D," I said.

"I am," Lucas replied, "but I also like to keep my worlds separate."

Shu typed something into her phone and then held it up for Lucas to read.

"The Pixel Pioneers?" He shook his head. "Nice try, Shu, but most people are so ignorant, they'll probably think we're pilgrims or something. "

"What about the Arcade Avengers?" I said.

"No to 'Arcade' and double no to 'Avengers,'" Lucas replied. "In the first case, arcades haven't existed for decades. As for the 'Avengers' part, everyone will think we're trying to rip off Marvel."

I couldn't believe what was happening. This was *my* squad, and coming up with a name for it had been *my* idea. How had Lucas suddenly become the only person who could greenlight an idea?

As my brain raced to come up with a name that had even a remote hope of pleasing His Majesty, Darian spoke up. "How about the Gaming Gurus?" he asked, smiling as if he thought he had just nailed it. Of *course* he would come up with a name like that. "Guru" is another name for an enlightened spiritual teacher, especially in religions that focus on meditation.

"That's not bad," Lucas admitted.

My jaw fell open in shock. What was so great about it? Why had he rejected both of my ideas—not to mention Shu's—but the minute Darian opened his mouth, Lucas was all over it?

"But to be honest, I've never been a big fan of the word 'guru,'" Lucas added, which made me feel a tiny bit better. "It feels like it sticks in the back of my throat." He said "guru" a few times to demonstrate, exaggerating his pronunciation more and more each time until the word lost all meaning, and it sounded like he really did have something stuck in the back of his throat.

"I have another one," Darian said. "The Level Legends." In fact, I like this one even better because it has a double meaning—video games have levels, and to win consistently, you need to be level headed." He looked around at the rest of us with his hands out as if he was just waiting for us to acknowledge his brilliance.

"I like where you're going with that," Lucas said, "and your instincts are spot on. But you see, Rumble Royale doesn't really have levels. And there's another popular game called League of Legends, so there's that too. Too much potential for brand confusion."

"Okay, Einstein," I said, not caring if my frustration was starting to show. "You've shot down all our ideas. What's your brilliant suggestion?"

Lucas grinned. "I thought you'd never ask." Then he just continued to sit there, a goofy smile stretched across his face.

"Well, what is it?" I said, my exasperation growing.

In response, Lucas leaped to his feet and held his hands up, spreading them in the air in dramatic fashion like a Hollywood director announcing the name of his next big movie: "The Stream Team."

He stood there with his arms wide, waiting for the rest of us to respond. When we didn't, he jumped into an explanation, as I knew he would.

"We're a team, right? That part should be obvious."

It was.

"As for the 'stream' part, that's ultimately what you want to become, right, Wyatt? A streamer, a content creator who doesn't just win games but who also broadcasts those wins to your millions of adoring fans? So, why not work your end goal into our team's name? Plus, the rhyme of 'stream' and 'team' has a certain aesthetic appeal, don't you think? Stream Team. You hear that?"

Aesthetic what? What was he talking about? Where was a dictionary or a thesaurus when I needed one?

Darian sat back in his chair and steepled his fingers as he stared at my RGB lights, which were slowly morphing between colors on the ceiling. "Yes, the name is rather elegant," he said, "not to mention that a stream bubbling over rocks is one of the most soothing and meditative sounds there is." He sat forward, his eyes flashing with excitement. "I like it! Shu, what do you think?"

"Stream Team," she said, nodding and giving him a thumbs-up. "Yes!"

THE STREAM TEAM

I took a deep breath and sighed. This squad was my idea, and I was the one who had recruited everyone, so why did it already feel like I was losing control of it? It wasn't that I disliked the name. I just wished the idea had come from anyone but Lucas—preferably from me—but try as I might, I couldn't come up with anything better.

"Shall we put it to a vote?" Lucas asked, rushing the rest of us along, as always, which was probably his way of making sure we had no time to object. He raised his hand, as did Darian and Shu, then all three of them looked at me.

"Are you sure you don't want to get this part in writing too?" I asked, my voice dripping with sarcasm, but Lucas didn't seem to notice—or at least, he didn't care.

"Oh, I will," he assured me. "Just one more reason to delay signing that contract, so I can add this as an amendment. But a simple show of hands will do for the moment."

"Fine," I said, letting out a huge huff of air. "The Stream Team it is."

Inside, I vowed that would be the last time I

would allow Lucas to railroad us into going along with his agenda. But who was I kidding? This was Lucas Maxwell I was talking about, the guy who claimed he had created an algorithm to win every potential *Warhammer* scenario. I just hoped he hadn't created a similar algorithm to win every potential argument against the rest of us—although I wouldn't have put it past him. As long as he focused that energy on helping us devise a strategy to win at *Rumble Royale,* though, I decided I would just have to find a way to live with it.

- 16 -

Once everyone had gone home and I was all alone in my gaming room, I sat in my chair and spun it back and forth as I stared up at the shifting lights on my ceiling, reflecting on everything that had happened over the past week. As frustrated as I was with some of Lucas's antics, as impatient as I became with Darian's obsession with mindfulness, and as mysterious as I found Shu, I had to admit that, so far, my plan was working.

Not everything had gone my way. The fact that Lucas's name for our squad had won out still bugged the heck out of me. But like that quote from

Confucius, I wasn't going to let a little failure like that stand between me and the video game fame and glory that I was dreaming about. There was no way I was going to live an ordinary life.

As I sat forward in my chair and booted up my console, I thought about the other quote, the one Darian brought up about discouragement and failure being the stepping stones to success. While I waited for the *Rumble Royale* lobby to fill, I just hoped I wouldn't have to learn that lesson too often.

Or too soon.

"Whatcha doin'?" Olivia asked as she came down the stairs, offering her signature greeting whenever she intruded on my space. When she reached the bottom of the stairs, she stopped and stared in disappointment. "Aw, did all your friends go home?"

"What does it look like?" I asked.

"Just kidding," she said. "I knew from Snap Maps that they were already gone."

I spun my chair toward her. "Don't tell me you already have Lucas and Darian on Snapchat too."

She looked down at the floor and shrugged.

THE STREAM TEAM

That girl didn't waste any time!

"Well, I don't want you pestering them. They're *my* friends, remember?"

Olivia looked up at me. "That doesn't mean they can't be my friends too!" For a second I thought I saw a flicker of pain in her eyes, and suddenly, I felt guilty. All she was trying to do was be nice.

"You're right," I admitted. "Sorry. I'm just a little stressed out. In case you haven't noticed, Lucas can be quite the handful."

"Tell me about it," she said. "You should see his Instagram feed."

She was already following him on Instagram, too? I really needed to get up to speed on my social media connections.

"So, you guys are actually gonna try to go pro at Rumble Royale, hey?" she said.

"Something like that," I replied. "But keep that to yourself for now, all right? I don't even want Mom and Dad knowing about it yet. And definitely don't post about it!"

"Why would I?" she said. "None of my friends care about your boring life anyway."

We were both silent for a moment.

"Want to know what our squad is called?" I ventured, wanting to test drive the name on someone outside the group.

"Sure."

"The Stream Team. Sounds terrible, right?"

I was really hoping she wouldn't like it, which would give me ammunition to get the rest of the team to reconsider. Instead, she smiled. "I think it's great." Then she looked down and toed the carpet. "I sure wish I knew how to play Rumble Royale."

My eyes widened in surprise. "You? I thought you hated video games."

"I don't hate them," she said. "I just hate the fact that you spend so much time down here gaming. You and I hardly ever get to hang out any more like we used to."

By that point, I was *really* feeling guilty.

"But if Shu's into it," she continued, "how bad could it be?"

I sat and stared at Olivia for a moment, seeing her in a new light.

"You know what? If you like, I can do a walk-through with you, just like I did with Shu and the others. Then you'll have a better idea of what the game's all about."

"Really?" she said, her face brightening. "That would be cool. It'll also give me something to talk to Shu about."

"Pull up a chair," I said as I reached forward to boot up my console. She grabbed my old gaming chair and plunked herself into it, rolling it right next to mine.

"You know, Wyatt, now that you're showing me

how to game and all, maybe one day I really can have a dance party down here with my friends."

I arched my left eyebrow and shot her a wry look, my lips twisted into a half grin. "Let's not get too carried away just yet..."

Continue the story with book 2!

Made in the USA
Monee, IL
22 June 2024